PLACE DE L.

MADELINE

MADELINE

story & pictures by
Ludwig Bemelmans

VIKING

VIKING
Published by the Penguin Group
Viking Penguin, a division of Penguin Books USA Inc.,
375 Hudson Street, New York, New York 10014, U.S.A.
Penguin Books Ltd, 27 Wrights Lane, London W8 5TZ, England
Penguin Books Australia Ltd, Ringwood, Victoria, Australia
Penguin Books Canada Ltd, 10 Alcorn Avenue, Toronto, Ontario, Canada M4V 3B2
Penguin Books (N.Z.) Ltd, 182-190 Wairau Road, Auckland 10, New Zealand
Penguin Books Ltd, Registered Offices: Harmondsworth, Middlesex, England

First published by The Viking Press, 1939
This edition published by Viking Penguin, a division of Penguin Books USA Inc.,
1992
9 10
Copyright © Ludwig Bemelmans, 1939
Copyright © renewed 1967 by Madeleine Bemelmans and Barbara Marciano
All rights reserved
Printed in Hong Kong
Set in Bodoni

MADELINE

In an old house in Paris
that was covered with vines

lived twelve little girls in two straight lines.

In two straight lines they broke their bread

and brushed their teeth

and went to bed.

They smiled at the good

and frowned at the bad

and sometimes they were very sad.

They left the house
at half past nine
in two straight lines

in rain

or shine—

the smallest one was Madeline.

She was not afraid of mice—

she loved winter, snow, and ice.

To the tiger in the zoo
Madeline just said, "Pooh-pooh,"

and nobody knew so well
how to frighten Miss Clavel.

In the middle of one night
Miss Clavel turned on her light
and said, "Something is not right!"

Little Madeline sat in bed,
cried and cried; her eyes were red.

And soon after Dr. Cohn
came, he rushed out to the phone

and he dialed: DANton-ten-six—

"Nurse," he said, "it's an appendix!"

Everybody had to cry—
not a single eye was dry.

Madeline was in his arm
in a blanket safe and warm.

In a car with a red light
they drove out into the night.

Madeline woke up two hours
later, in a room with flowers.

Madeline soon ate and drank.
On her bed there was a crank,

and a crack on the ceiling had the habit
of sometimes looking like a rabbit.

Outside were birds, trees, and sky—
and so ten days passed quickly by.

One nice morning Miss Clavel said—
"Isn't this a fine—

day to visit

Madeline."

VISITORS FROM TWO TO FOUR
read a sign outside her door.

Tiptoeing with solemn face,
with some flowers and a vase,

in they walked and then said, "Ahhh,"
when they saw the toys and candy
and the dollhouse from Papa.

But the biggest surprise by far—
on her stomach
was a scar!

"Good-by," they said, "we'll come again,"

and the little girls left in the rain.

They went home and broke their bread

brushed their teeth

and went to bed.

In the middle of the night
Miss Clavel turned on the light
and said, "Something is not right!"

And afraid of a disaster

Miss Clavel ran fast

and faster,

and she said, "Please children do—
tell me what is troubling you?"

And all the little girls cried, "Boohoo,
we want to have our appendix out, too!"

"Good night, little girls!
Thank the lord you are well!
And now go to sleep!"
said Miss Clavel.

And she turned out the light—

and closed the door—

and that's all there is—

there isn't any more.

HERE is a list for those who may wish
to identify the Paris scenes Ludwig
Bemelmans has pictured in this book.

On the cover and in one of the
illustrations
THE EIFFEL TOWER

In the picture of the lady feeding
the horse
THE OPERA

A gendarme chases a jewel thief across
THE PLACE VENDOME

A wounded soldier at
THE HOTEL DES INVALIDES

A rainy day in front of
NOTRE DAME

A sunny day looking across
THE GARDENS AT THE LUXEMBOURG

Behind the little girls skating is
THE CHURCH OF THE SACRE COEUR

A man is feeding birds in
THE TUILERIES GARDENS FACING
THE LOUVRE

PLACE DE LA

NCORDE